Rave Alone!

A Coming of Age Story

Rave Alone!
A Coming of Age Story

The Original Screenplay

Macarena Luz Bianchi

Imprint

Spark Social, Inc.

Rave Alone! A Coming of Age Story: The Original Screenplay

Subscribe to the email list for this book spark.fyi/rascript

Spark Social, Inc.
Miami, FL USA
sparksocialpress.com

ISBN: 978-1-954489-00-4
Ebook: 978-1-954489-01-1

Printed Edition 2020 | Script 2001
Rave Alone! Series

Dedication

To those who have ever been moved by music and have found connection and inspiration within the diverse dance floor of life.

Contents

Synopsis

Miami 2001

After blackmailing his older sister, Alyssa, into taking him to a rave, 15-year-old Robbie leaves his sheltered home to be exposed to the electronic music and party scene. Upon entering the nine-acre ULTRA Music Festival, Robbie gets separated from Alyssa and her friends, forcing him to take responsibility and make his own decisions for the first time.

What starts as a mere party turns into a quest that drives Robbie to empower himself to new heights. He befriends eccentrics, makes the scariest of enemies, and has his eyes uncovered to a new world. Robbie sets out on an unexpected adventure to find his sister. What he finds instead is himself.

Rating: N/A
Running Time: N/A

Screenplay

R A V E   A L O N E !

By Macarena Luz Bianchi

House music plays. Fade In:

Miami

2001

EXT - SUBURBAN HOUSE - MORNING

Robbie, 15-year-old, and Alyssa, 18-year-old, stand in their driveway as their parents rush in and out of the house, putting luggage in a car.

                    MOM
          (on her way in the house)
          ...and don't forget to lock
          the doors...
          (on her way out of the house)
          ...make sure you leave some
          lights on at night so that
          the house doesn't look
          abandoned...
               (on her way in)
          ...and don't forget to feed
          Boomer...

Dad closes the trunk. Mom puts her purse in the car and stands in front of her kids.

                    MOM (CONTÍD)
          Alyssa, please take care of
          Robbie. Remember, he's
          younger than you.

                    ALYSSA
          Yes, mom.

                    ROBBIE
          I can take care of myself.

                    MOM
          Of course you can pumpkin.

Mom reaches over and hugs him. Robbie is
uncomfortable.

                    MOM
          Behave and listen to your
          sister. And do your homework,
          okay?

Robbie pulls back, annoyed.

                    MOM (CONTÍD)
                (to Alyssa)
          There's money in the kitchen.
          Don't spend it all the first
          day. There's extra in case of
          any emergency.
          That does not include new
          shoes. There's plenty of
          food. Make sure he eats
          something other than junk
          food.
                    ALYSSA
          Yes, mom

                    Mom

Um, what am I forgetting?

                    DAD

Nothing. They're going to be
fine. Right, guys?

                    ALYSSA
          Yup.

                    DAD
          Robbie, you're the man of the
          house now so YOU take care of
          your sister.

Alyssa snorts in amusement.

Dad kisses the kids and rushes to the
driver's seat.

                    DAD (CONTÍD)
          Come on, love, we're going to
          get traffic.

                    MOM
          Alright, you guys take care
          of each other.

Mom hugs both kids and gets into the car.
She rolls down the window.

                    MOM (CONTÍD)
          I'll call you when we get
          there. Number's on the
          fridge.

Car pulls back out of the driveway as Mom
continues to talk.

                    MOM (CONTÍD)
          Call in case of an emergency,
          for anything. Call! I love
          you!

Alyssa and Robbie wave as the car pulls

away.

                         ALYSSA
              Just stay out of my way.

Robbie rushes past her, almost knocking her
over on his way in the house.

                         ROBBIE
                       (laughing)
              No problem.

Alyssa walks in and closes the door behind
her.

                                        CUT TO:
INT. - HOUSE LIVING ROOM - LATER

Robbie is in front of the TV, playing video
games. The doorbell rings.

OFFSCREEN:

                         ALYSSA
              Hey.

                         PAZ
              Hello, hello DJ Lloyd. Music
              heaven here we come!

                         ALYSSA
              What?

                         PAZ
                       (loudly)
              I got the ULTRA tickets!

                    ALYSSA

          What?

                     PAZ
               SHHH!

Voices mumble. Robbie smiles as he turns off
his game. He gets up and heads into the
kitchen.
                                   CUT TO:

INT - HOUSE KITCHEN -DAY

Alyssa and PAZ, 18 year-old, are at the
counter.

Alyssa quickly shoves the tickets under a
magazine.

                         ROBBIE
               ULTRA? I don't remember you
               asking Mom and Dad to go to a
               RAVE?
                    (to Paz) Oh,
               hello Paz.

               ALYSSA
               Shut up, Robbie.

               PAZ
               It's not a rave. It's
               an electronic music
               festival. Like a
               concert.

                    ROBBIE
          Riiight.
          (to Alyssa)
          You know, Dad said I'm_supposed
          to take care of you and I don't
          think I can let you go.

                    ALYSSA
          let me..? This is none of
          your business. Why don't you
          go jerk off to one of those
          web sites you're always on
          and leave us alone.

                    ROBBIE
               (embarrassed)
          I don't know what...if
          you go, I'm going to
          have to tell.

                    ALYSSA
               (to Paz)
          Can you believe this crap?

                    PAZ
          Come on. You're not really
          going to tell?

                    ROBBIE
          Hell yeah.

                    ALYSSA

          AGH!

Alyssa throws the magazine at Robbie's head.

                    ROBBIE
          Violence will get you
          nowhere.

                    ALYSSA
          Alright, I'll give you fifty
          bucks.

                    ROBBIE
          Nope.

                    ALYSSA
          A hundred.

          You little shit.
Robbie pulls the paper with his parents'
number off the fridge and waves it around.
                    ROBBIE
          I think Mom would definitely
          consider this an emergency.
Alyssa lunges for him. Robbie steps back,
laughing.

                    ALYSSA
          Okay, what do you want?

                    ROBBIE
               (Pauses)
          I want to go with you.

                    ALYSSA
          Go where?
                    ROBBIE
          Ultra.

                    PAZ
          Ha! What do you know about
          dance music?

                    ROBBIE
          Whatever. I want to go.

                    ALYSSA
          NO fucking way!

EXT - BAYFRONT PARK - DAY
Alyssa, Paz, and Robbie approach the
entrance to Bayfront Park. Robbie looks
intimidated.

A young man, ANDY, walks up to them.

                    ANDY
          Hello, ladies! Robbie!

                    ROBBIE
          You didn't say *she* was coming.

                    ANDY
               (taunting)
          Oh, yes, baby, I'm with you
          ALL day long.
               (to Alyssa)
          I can't believe we're stuck
          baby-sitting.

                    PAZ
          Okay, I printed copies of the
          schedule.

She hands a copy to Andy and Alyssa. Robbie
holds out his hand but Paz just waves him
off.

                    PAZ (CONTÍD)
               (to Andy and Alyssa)
          All the DJ's we have to see
          with the stage number and
          times.

They start to walk towards entrance.
Andy folds his schedule and tosses it into a

garbage can.

                    ALYSSA
          Hurry up.

                    ROBBIE
          Did you bring money?

                    ALYSSA
          Yes.

                    ROBBIE
          Hand it over.

                    ALYSSA
          No, you'll lose it. I'll hold
          it.

                    PAZ
          DJ Lloyd is going to be at
          stage 5. You excited, Al?

                    ALYSSA
               (blushing)
          He's so cute!

                    PAZ
          And talented.

                    ANDY
          I'd do him.

                    ROBBIE
               (interrupting)
          Excuse me! What if you lose
          it?

                    ALYSSA
          I won't.

                    ROBBIE
          What if you do?

                    ALYSSA

                    (agitated)
          Robbie, shut up!

                    ROBBIE
          How many people are here!?!

Andy puts his arm around Robbie.

                    ANDY
          A lot. So, stay close.

Robbie steps away quickly. Robbie pulls
Alyssa aside.

                    ROBBIE
          Keep that fag away from me!

                    ALYSSA
                    (annoyed)
          Get over yourself.

EXT BAYFRONT PARK ENTRANCE - DAY

They enter the Park. There are people
everywhere.

Robbie lags behind the group, checking
everyone out that walks by.

A well-endowed girl, with little on, walks
by and Robbie stops to get a good look.

He smiles and turns back. The group is not
there. Robbie begins to look around
anxiously.

                    ROBBIE
          Alyssa? Alyssa?

Robbie becomes nervous and begins to run
around.

CUT TO:

EXT - BAYFRONT PARK - DAY

Alyssa stops and notices Robbie is missing.

                    ALYSSA
          Where is he?

Paz and Andy stop and look around.

                    ANDY
          He was just here.

The group begins to look around for him.

                    PAZ
          Come on, Alyssa. I don't want
          to miss anyone!

                    ALYSSA
          (worried)
          I have to find him. My
          parents will kill me.

                    ANDY
          You   didn't   lose   him.   He's
          around   here   somewhere.   Let's
          go back by the entrance.

They walk towards the entrance.

EXT - PARK WATER BOOTH - DAY

CUT TO:

Robbie comes up to a water booth. He's
sweating from running around.

                    ROBBIE (CONTÍD)
          How much for a water?

                    VENDOR

14

                    Six bucks, kid.

Robbie opens his wallet and counts four
dollars.
He steps away from the booth and begins to
look around nervously.

EXT - PARK - DAY

Robbie walks up to Police officer
who is walking around.

                    ROBBIE
          Uh, yeah, I'm lost. Can you
          help me find my sister?

                    OFFICER
               (Shaking his head)
          In this place? You have to be
          joking?

                    ROBBIE
          Don't you help people?

                    OFFICER
          Look, kid, stand by the
          entrance and wait for them to
          leave.

                    ROBBIE
          What time does this end?

                    OFFICER
               (shrugging)
          It goes on all night.

                    ROBBIE
          So that's it? Wait all night
          by the entrance?

                    OFFICER
          What do you want me to do?

                    ROBBIE
          I don't know. Walkie-talkie
          somebody. Isn't there a loud
          speaker or something?

Shady guy, a Drug Dealer, wearing a backpack
walks by and looks back at the cop.

                    OFFICER
          You joking?

                    ROBBIE
          Never mind.

Robbie turns around and looks around not
knowing where to go.

Drug Dealer, hands off to another guy.

Drug Dealer stands around, counting and

pocketing cash. He is next to a stage, his

backpack at his feet.

OFFICER, observing him, calls him over.

Drug Dealer pushes bag under stage with his
foot, takes a deep breath, and walks over to
the officer who begins to question him.

Robbie, wandering about, runs into JUANA,
drag queen.

                    ROBBIE (CONTÍD)
          Excuse me.
Robbie notices Juana and is immediately
panic stricken.

                    JUANA
          Is okay.
          (checking him out)
          Allo, sweet thing.

Robbie walks away quickly. He backs into

stage. Foot hits backpack. Robbie looks
around and picks it up. He opens it and
finds 3 bottles of water, a pack of gum, and
a box of mints.

                    ROBBIE
              (mumbling to himself)
          Hate mints... Al likes them,
          if I ever find that bitch.

He looks around again, pockets the gum and
the mints, puts bag on his shoulder, and
walks away.

Drug Dealer, still talking to officer sees
him take backpack.

EXT - PARK - DAY

Robbie walks up to the VIP Guest Services
booth.

                    ROBBIE
          Hi, I'm lost. I need help
          finding my sister.

VIP person waves a badge in his face.

                    VIP PERSON
          Are you VIP?

                    ROBBIE
          I don't think so.

                    VIP PERSON
          Well, this is guest services
          for VIP only.

                    ROBBIE
          But I'm...How do I become
          VIP?

                    VIP PERSON

Either you are a special guest
or you pay a hundred and
twenty-five dollars.

                    ROBBIE
A hundred?

                    VIP PERSON
And twenty-five.

                    ROBBIE
At a rave?

                    VIP PERSON
                    (annoyed)
This is not a rave.

                    ROBBIE
Okay.

Robbie walks away.

EXT - PARK - DAY

Alyssa walking about frantically.

Andy leans up against a booth looking bored.
Paz checks her schedule.

                    ANDY
Can we take our pills now?

                    ALYSSA
No. I'm not taking anything
until we find him.

                    PAZ
You ARE going to take them?
HELLO? He'll tell your Mom
and she'll tell mine. There's
no way she would believe I

don't.

                    ANDY
          Ah, stop worrying. He won't
          even notice.

                                        CUT TO:

                    PAZ
          Right. My mom was watching
          some special on ecstasy and
          she asked me if it was like
          crack.

                    ALYSSA
               (ignoring Paz)
          We need to find him *before* we
          take them, Andy.

                    ANDY
          Okay, let's go look for him.

                    PAZ
          According to the schedule we
          need to be at stage two in
          ten minutes. I am not missing
          this.

                    ANDY
          Don't worry. None of the good
          dj's come on till later.

                    PAZ
          They are all good. Or they
          wouldn't be here!

Andy grabs Paz's arm and leads her. They all
start walking around.

                                        CUT TO:

EXT - PARK - DAY

Robbie is standing still watching people

dance. He drinks water.

Rolly, big steroid guy, is drinking beer
with his friends.

Rolly trips and bumps into Robbie, dropping
his beer.

                    ROLLY
          What the fuck?

                    ROBBIE
          I'm sorry.

                    ROLLY
          Shit, I'll make you sorry you
          little fuck. You need to buy
          me another beer.

                    ROBBIE
          Sorry, I don't have any
          money.

                    ROLLY
          No money? Well what the fuck
          do you have here?

Rolly pulls backpack away from Robbie. He
opens it.

                    ROLLY (CONTÍD)
          Water? You rolling?

                    ROBBIE
          What?

                    ROLLY
          Tell YOU what, I keep this. I
          let you live.

Rolly throws a bottle of water to one of his
friends.

                    ROLLY (CONTÍD)
          Now get the fuck out of here.

Robbie walks away, still looking around
frantically.

EXT - PARK -DAY

Exhausted, Robbie sits down. He looks around.
He puts his head down. When he looks up, he
notices a security guard.

EXT - PARK -DAY

Robbie walks over to him.

The Security Guard is leaning against a
booth, checking out some young girls
dancing.

                    ROBBIE
          Hey, listen, I lost my
          sister. Could you help me
          out?

                    GUARD
          What do you want me to do?
          Why don't you call her?

                    ROBBIE
          I don't have a phone.

Guard reaches and pulls out his phone. He
offers it to Robbie.

                    ROBBIE (CONTÍD)
          She doesn't have a phone.

                    GUARD
          Well, that's your problem
          right there. You need to keep

up with the times. I mean,
even my grandmother has a
cell phone.

                    ROBBIE
Okay, so I'm low tech. You
can't help me?

                    GUARD
It's more of a safety
measure. You see the
situation you're in now. It
wouldn't even exist if
everyone just kept up with
technology.

He flips open his phone and shows it to
Robbie.

                    GUARD (CONTÍD)
Look at this, I can even
check my email, send email,
check the weather. Whatever.
And I would never lose
anyone.

                    ROBBIE
Look, I get it but...

                    GUARD
What you need to do is go and
get yourself a phone. And get
your sister one while you're
at it.
They have a booth around here
somewhere.

                    ROBBIE
Yeah, thanks a lot.

                    GUARD
Any time, buddy.

Robbie walks away from the guard.

EXT - PARK - DAY

Robbie begins to wander about. He comes to
KILLER LIFE T-shirt stand. Checks them out
in amazement.

Behind Robbie, we see Drug Dealer steps in
frame. He yells at him.

                    DRUG DEALER
          Hey! Kid!

Robbie, confused, jumps and begins to run
away.

                    DRUG DEALER (CONTÍD)
          Get the fuck back here.

Drug Dealer proceeds to chase Robbie through
the park. Robbie dodges into a crowd of
people dancing.
He finally loses the Drug Dealer.

                                        CUT TO:

EXT - PARK - DAY

Alyssa looks frantic.

Paz is still checking her schedule. Andy is
lying on the floor.

                    ANDY
                 (whining)
          We should drop soon.

                    ALYSSA

          I told you. I'm not doing
          anything until I find him!

A CAMERA GUY comes up to them.

                    CAMERA GUY
          Hey, Can I take your picture?

                    ANDY
          Sure!

The three get together. Andy poses and Paz
smiles. Alyssa looks around distracted.
The camera guy prints the card and shows it
to them.

The card reads LET'S GET DOWN and has
the picture of them printed on it.

                    CAMERA GUY (CONTÍD)
          Nice, huh? Only ten bucks.

                    ANDY
          Ten bucks?

Andy waves him away. Camera guy walks away.

                    PAZ
          I can't believe I'm missing
          this. Alyssa, we are on a
          tight schedule.

                    ALYSSA
          Yeah? Well, if you had
          bothered to make one of those
          for that SHIT than maybe he
          would know how to find us,
          huh?

Paz looks away, upset.

                    ANDY
          It's not her fault. It's not

                    anyone's fault. Let's just
                    take our pills and have some
                    fun.

                         ALYSSA
                    NO! Are you deaf?

                         ANDY
                    That little, homophobic shit
                    is not going to ruin my
                    party!

                         ALYSSA
                    You can take your damn pill
                    whenever YOU want. I'm going
                    to keep looking. Okay?

                         ANDY
                    Don't be a bitch!

Alyssa screams out.

                                             CUT TO:

EXT - PARK - DAY

Robbie stops running. He sits down on the
floor. He screams out.

EXT - PARK - DAY

Alyssa looks around.

                         ALYSSA
                    Did you hear that?

EXT - PARK - DAY

Robbie stands up and looks around.

Juana walks over to Robbie.

                    JUANA

     How you doing?
Robbie looks up surprised. He jumps back.

                    JUANA (CONTÍD)
          Don't worry. I not going to
          hurt you, baby.
                                   CUT TO:
                    ROBBIE
                    (mumbling)
          I thought you were someone
          else.

                    JUANA
          Are you disappointed?

                    ROBBIE
          No, actually I'm...

                    JUANA
          What are you doing here all
          by yourself?

                    ROBBIE
                    (mumbling)
          I thought you were someone else.

                    JUANA
          Are you disappointed?

                    ROBBIE
          No, actually I'm...

                    JUANA
          What are you doing here all
          by yourself?

                    ROBBIE
          I'm here with my sister and
          some of her friends but now I
          can't find them.

                    JUANA
          Ay, you're lost!

Juana puts her arm around Robbie.

                    JUANA (CONTÍD)
          Come here, baby, you stay
          with me. What you say your
          name is?
                    ROBBIE
               (nervously)
          Robbie.
Juana leads him to three large men in muscle
t-shirts.
                    JUANA
          Robbie, this is Alex, Ivan, y
          Carlos. Boys this is my
          friend, Robbie.

Robbie shakes hands with all of them.

Ivan offers Robbie some water. Robbie
accepts.

                    ROBBIE
          Thanks.

                    JUANA
          Honey, you take drinks from
          strangers?

                    ROBBIE
          Huh?

                    JUANA
Your mama never told you not
to drink from strangers.

                    ROBBIE
Well, yeah. I just thought...

                    ROBBIE
               (nodding)
Okay.

                    JUANA
Are you having fun?

                    ROBBIE
Not really.

                    JUANA
Why not?

                    ROBBIE
Long story.

                    JUANA
Tell me, maybe I can help.

Robbie sits down with Juana at a table,
drinking water, telling his story.

                    ROBBIE
... some lunatic has been
chasing me around the entire
place.

                    JUANA
Who is he?

                    ROBBIE
I don't know. But he's a big
guy.

                    JUANA
          Is he cute?

Robbie shrugs. He looks around.

                    ROBBIE
          If I don't find her soon,
          she'll kill me.

                    JUANA
          She worry about you?

                    ROBBIE
          I doubt it. She hates me.

Juana reaches over and grabs his face.

                    JUANA
          NO, who could hate a face
          like this?

                    ROBBIE
          She does. I had to blackmail
          her into bringing me here.

                    JAUNA
          Brothers can be VERY
          difficult. My brother was
          very mean to me when we were
          little. He use to make fun of
          me all the time. And he used
          to let his friends beat me up
          for fun.

                    ROBBIE
          Really?
                    JUANA
          Yes.

                    ROBBIE
          Are you guys close now?

                    JUANA
          We were but he does not speak
          to me anymore. We had a very
          bad fight a year ago and I
          don't see him again. He has a
          son, my godson, Juan Carlos.

                    ROBBIE
          Do you miss him?

                    JUANA
          Very much.

                    ROBBIE
          So, why don't you call him?

                    JUANA
          What if he don't want to talk
          to me?

                    ROBBIE
          At least you'll know. I don't
          think I would ever not talk
          to my sister. No matter how
          much of a bitch she was. And
          she is a bitch.

                    JUANA
          You be nice to your sister.
          We girls can be very
          sensitive.

Robbie smiles in amusement.

                    ROBBIE

If I ever see her again.

                    JUANA
          You no worry. I promise
          everything will be fine.
          You'll find her.

                    ROBBIE
          Hey, thanks for helping me
          out. What's your name?

Juana stands up and dramatically curtsies.

                    JUANA
          My name is Juana.

                    ROBBIE
              (Mumbling)
          Juana.

Juana sits back down and takes out a pack of
cigarettes.

                    ROBBIE (CONTÍD)
          Juana, but you're a guy,
          right?

Juana laughs.

                    JUANA
          I am more woman than you
          would know what to do with,
          honey.

Robbie laughs with a confused look on his
face.

Juana offers him a cigarette. Robbie takes
one. Juana lights it and then hers. Robbie
begins to cough immediately and puts it out.

Juana laughs.

                    JUANA (CONTÍD)
          Better not to start... like
          coffee or crack, you know?

Robbie laughs and coughs.

                    ROBBIE
          Yeah!

Robbie stands up.

                    ROBBIE (CONTÍD)
          Well, I really have to go
          look for them.

Juana stands up.

                    JUANA
          Well, baby, you come look for
          me if you need anything.

Juana reaches over and pulls Robbie into a
hug. Robbie hugs her back.
          Thanks. ROBBIE

                    JUANA
          Thank you.

Robbie waves at Alex, Ivan, and Carlos. They

wave back. Robbie walks away, looking

around.

EXT - PARK -DAY

Robbie walks. The camera guy comes up to
him.

                    CAMERA GUY
          Want to buy a card?

Camera guy hands him a couple of cards. It
reads: LET'S GET DOWN and has the picture of
Paz, Andy, and Alyssa.

                    ROBBIE
          Where did you take this? I'm
          looking for them.

                    CAMERA GUY
          I don't remember. You want it
          or not?

                    ROBBIE
          This is my sister. Can I have
          it?

                    CAMERA GUY
          That's ten bucks, kid.

                    ROBBIE
          I have four dollars.

                    CAMERA GUY
          Ten bucks.

                    ROBBIE
          Who's going to buy a picture
          of complete strangers?

                    CAMERA GUY
          Listen, kid you want to
          pay the ten bucks or
          what? You're wasting my
          time.

                    ROBBIE
          Never mind.

Robbie hands the card back and the camera
guy walks away.

EXT - PARK - DAY

Robbie sees another kid from school, a
senior and bully.

                    ROBBIE
                 (to himself)
          Shit.

Robbie tries to turn but Senior sees him.

                    SENIOR
          Hey, you go to my school?

Robbie turns to face Senior.

                    ROBBIE
          Uh, yeah. We have the same
          lunch.

Senior is very aggressive in his speech.

Robbie is intimidated by the Senior's
unpredictability.

                    SENIOR
                 (loudly)
          No!
                 (softly)
          No way man.

Robbie doesn't know what to do.

                    SENIOR (CONTÍD)
          (seriously) What the FUCK!
          (smiling) You doing here?

                    ROBBIE
          Ahhh, just checking out some
          DJ's.

                    SENIOR
          FUCK!

Robbie is startled.

                    SENIOR (CONTÍD)
          I LOVE this music.

Senior notices something in the distance.

                    SENIOR (CONT'D)
          Cool man! Gotta go.
          See you at school, man.

Senior reaches his hand and Robbie shakes

it. Robbie stands there, confused.

EXT - PARK - DAY

Alyssa, Paz, and Andy walk and look around.

EXT - PARK -DAY

Robbie sneaks onto a stage.

He looks for them in the crowd.

As he exits on one side, Paz steps on stage
on the other she's suppose to be looking at
the crowd, but the DJ mesmerizes her.

Alyssa and Andy signal her to look around
from the dance floor.

EXT - PARK -DAY

Robbie walks past a group of people dancing.

Girl stumbles by him and begins to puke on
his shoe.

Robbie steps back and is grabbed by his
shirt collar. He's turned around by the
Drug Dealer.

                    DRUG DEALER
          Where is it you little fuck?

                    ROBBIE
          What?

                    DRUG DEALER
          My backpack. I saw you take
          it.

                    ROBBIE
          Your ?...

He shakes his head.

                    ROBBIE (CONTÍD)
          I don't have it.

Drug Dealer begins to shake him.

                    DRUG DEALER
          Don't lie to me. I saw you.

                    ROBBIE
          Yeah, I di...didn't know it
          was yours. I was thirsty and
          then this guy spilled his
          beer and then...HE has your
          backpack.

                    DRUG DEALER
          One more time. Where is it?

                    ROBBIE
          Some guy took it from me.

                    DRUG DEALER
          Look, you little shit, that
          bag is worth more than your
          life but I would be willing
          to trade. You understand?

                    ROBBIE
          Okay, okay, I'll get it.
          Just...just let me..

Drug Dealer loosens his grip on Robbie.

Robbie takes off running.

Drug Dealer follows after him. Drug Dealer
chases him. Robbie loses Drug Dealer.

Robbie walks around, looking around him and
behind him, anxiously.

He trips over a record case. A man, LLOYD,
helps him up.

                    LLOYD
          You alright?

                    ROBBIE
          Yeah, yeah, I'm fine. Sorry
          about that.

                    LLOYD
          No problem. Give me a hand?

Lloyd motions to the cases of records next
to the stage.

                    ROBBIE
          Sure.

He helps carry a case on to the stage by the
                    DJ booth.

                    ROBBIE (CONTÍD)

                    You a DJ?

               LLOYD
          Yeah, Lloyd.

Lloyd reaches his hand out to Robbie.

               ROBBIE
          Robbie.

Robbie shakes his hand.

               ROBBIE (CONTÍD)
          Wait, are you DJ Lloyd?

               LLOYD
                (smiling)
          You like my music?

               ROBBIE
          No... I mean I haven't
          heard... but my sister talks
          about you all the time.

               LLOYD
          Really? Where she at?

               ROBBIE
          I wish I knew.

               LLOYD
          This place IS a mad house.

               ROBBIE
          No shit. I almost got my ass
          kicked twice today.

Girl comes up and asks him to sign CD
cover. Lloyd signs it and hands it back
to her.

               LLOYD
          You don't strike me as a
          troublemaker.

                    ROBBIE
Not me. There's assholes all
over the place.

                    LLOYD
You thirsty?

Lloyd reaches by the DJ booth and pulls two
bottles of water. He tosses one to Robbie.
Robbie opens his bottle and smells it.

Alright? LLOYD

                    ROBBIE
               (nodding)
Uh-huh. Thanks man.

They drink.
                    LLOYD
So what happened?

                    ROBBIE
I found this backpack of
water. I thought someone lost
it. And I didn't have any
money so I took it. But then
this asshole spilled his
drink all over me and then
took it. I didn't care cause
it wasn't mine. Except now
the owner is after me.

                    LLOYD
How old are you?

                    ROBBIE

Fifteen.

Lloyd sits down and offers a chair to
Robbie. Robbie sits down.

                    LLOYD
          Sounds like you got a
          problem.

                    ROBBIE
          Yeah. And I can't find my
          sister or her friends. She
          would know what to do.

                    LLOYD
          Well, you have two options.

Robbie nods his head. Two girls walk past
pointing and smiling at Lloyd.

                    LLOYD (CONTÍD)
          Either you go home and miss
          this party, or you go back to
          the asshole and get that guys
          bag back.

                    ROBBIE
          What? Are you crazy? That guy
          would kill me. And I can't
          get home, anyway. I have no
          money, no car...

                    LLOYD
          You can't run all day.

                    ROBBIE
          Why not? I've made it this
          far.

                    LLOYD
          Look, I'm just saying, the
          right thing would be for you to

get it back. Be a man. What's
the worse that could happen?

                ROBBIE
Uh, get my ass kicked?

                LLOYD
Exactly.

                ROBBIE
Easy for you to say. I bet no
one messes with you.
                LLOYD
          (laughing)
I've had my ass kicked. We've
all had.. at some point.

                ROBBIE
Maybe the cops could help?

                LLOYD
Maybe...

                ROBBIE
You think I'm a coward?

                LLOYD
Nah, just do what feels
right. You'll be fine.

Lloyd stands up. Robbie stands up.

                LLOYD (CONTÍD)
It was nice meeting you,
Robbie. I gotta set up.

                ROBBIE
Alright, thanks a lot, man.

They shake hands.

                LLOYD
Good luck.

                    ROBBIE
                 (nodding)
              Yeah, thanks.

Robbie walks away from the booth, still
looking around. He looks at his bottle of
water. He cracks his knuckles and begins
walking around with his head up, looking
around as though he's searching for someone
as opposed to avoiding someone.

EXT - PARK -EVENING

As he's walking, a beautiful blonde,
Sarah, 24 years old, comes running
towards him.

                    SARAH
              Hi, can I have some of your
              water?

                    ROBBIE
                 (stuttering)
              Ye-yeah. Sure. Here.

Robbie hands his bottle over. She goes to
drink it.

                    ROBBIE (CONTÍD)
              Aren't you gonna check it
              first?

                    SARAH
              Uh, *I* asked you for it.

                    ROBBIE
              Right, yeah, sorry.

She drinks and offers it back.

                    ROBBIE (CONTÍD)
          Keep it.

                    SARAH
          Thanks. I'm dying - it's hot.

Robbie nods. Sarah drinks more.

                    SARAH (CONTÍD)
          What's your name?

                    ROBBIE
          Robbie.

She sits down and motions for Robbie to sit
next to her.

                    SARAH
          I'm Sarah. You here alone?

                    ROBBIE
          Sort of. I came with my
          sister and her friends but I
          can't find them.

                    SARAH
          Ah, you poor thing. How old
          are you?

                    ROBBIE
          Fifteen.

                    SARAH
          Ah! You are SO adorable.

Robbie looks away, embarrassed. Sarah
laughs.

                    ROBBIE
          What?

                    SARAH
          Nothing. Isn't this great?
          You must have a cool sister.
          To bring you here. I love it!
          Such good music.
          Such good energy. It really
          moves me, you know?

Robbie nods.

                    SARAH (CONTÍD)
          And to be here at your age!
          Wow! I mean I didn't begin to
          appreciate this until a
          couple of years ago. I'm
          twenty-four, now. You're so
          lucky. You must be a really
          special guy. It's a real
          coming together of people. I
          mean there are the few
          assholes but mostly
          everybody's about the vibe,
          the music. You know.

Robbie nods.

                    SARAH (CONTÍD)
          I mean to have so many
          awesome DJ's here together
          pooling their talent to
          create this environment for
          us to feed off of? Amazing,
          right?

Robbie nods, laughing.

                    SARAH (CONTÍD)
What?

                    ROBBIE
You sure talk a lot.

                    SARAH
Oh, I'm sorry.

                    ROBBIE
No, no. It's great. It's
nice. I like hearing you
talk.

Robbie looks away, embarrassed.

                    SARAH
You know it's so great just
to be able to let loose and
dance like a maniac.

                    ROBBIE
                 (looking away)

Mmm.

                    SARAH
What?

                    ROBBIE
I don't really dance.

                    SARAH
How come?

                    ROBBIE
I don't know. I guess, I
don't really know how.

                    SARAH
          Know how? That's something
          you feel.

Robbie shrugs his shoulders.

                    SARAH (CONTÍD)
          Maybe you should try it
          sometime?

                    ROBBIE
          Maybe.

Sarah motions to a group of kids dancing.

                    ROBBIE (CONTÍD)
          Maybe later.

                    SARAH
               (laughing)
          You are so sweet. Do you have a
          girlfriend?

                    ROBBIE
          Nah.

Robbie shrugs his shoulders.

                    SARAH (CONTÍD)
          Do you like someone?

                    ROBBIE
          I did. She's going out with
          someone else.

                    SARAH
          Have you ever had a girlfriend?

                    ROBBIE
          Yeah, yeah, lots.

Sarah looks at him, questioningly.

                    ROBBIE (CONTÍD)
          No, not really. I mean, not a
          real girlfriend.

                    SARAH
          Why not?

                    ROBBIE
          I don't know. I never seem to
          say the right thing...

                    SARAH
          Well, let me just say, I
          think you're really cute and
          when you get to be my age
          girls will be throwing
          themselves at you.

                    ROBBIE
          Somehow, I doubt that.

                    SARAH
          Trust me. Do you have gum?

                    ROBBIE
          Actually, I do.

Robbie pulls out the pack of gum and offers
it to Sarah. Sarah takes a piece and hands
the pack back. He takes a piece, as well. He
pulls out the box of mints.

                    ROBBIE
          Mint?

                    SARAH
          No thanks, I hate mints. Too
          chalky right now.

                    ROBBIE
                  (mesmerized)
          Me, too!

                    SARAH
          So, anyway, like I was
          saying. What was I saying?

                    ROBBIE
                  (laughing)
          Something about me and girls?

                    SARAH
          Exactly. Girls don't really
          know what they want at your
          age but when they get a
          little older, they wise up.
          Just stay honest and true...
          do not lie or cheat. If you
          find a girl you connect with,
          don't blow it because that's
          really special, you know what
          I mean?

Robbie nods.

                    SARAH (CONTÍD)
          I mean my ex was a total
          jerk. I really loved him. But
          he totally didn't appreciate
          me at all. Why are men so
          afraid of expressing
          themselves?

                    ROBBIE
                  (confused)

I don't know.

                    SARAH
I mean, in the end, he
regretted it and tried to get
me back, but it was too late.
So, whose loss is it? His,
right?

                    SARAH
I mean, in the end, he
regretted it and tried to get
me back, but it was too late.
So, whose loss is it? His,
right?

Robbie nods, smiling.
                    ROBBIE
Definitely his.

                    SARAH
Now, I have a strict NO-
baggage rule.

                    ROBBIE
No baggage?

                    SARAH
Emotional baggage. No games,
no bullshit, no lies. Just
fun. It's either good or it's
NOT. Simple really.
Relationships are hard enough
without unnecessary crap.
Always be honest and don't
take shit from girls either.
Believe me, I know. We can be
drama queens.
Avoid drama. Life's too
short, you know?

                    ROBBIE
          Yeah.

                    SARAH
               (laughing)
          Am I talking nonsense?

                    ROBBIE
          No, you're probably the
          smartest girl I've ever met.

Sarah reaches over and puts Robbie's arm
around her.

                    SARAH
          Thanks, babe.

Sarah sighs in pleasure.

                    ROBBIE
          Can I ask you something
          without you getting mad?

                    SARAH
          No, I'm not a lesbian.

                    ROBBIE
          What?!

                    SARAH
          I'm kidding. What?

                    ROBBIE
          Oh, Are you, are you on
          anything?

                    SARAH
               (laughing)
          Is it that obvious?

                    ROBBIE
          No, you seem totally normal.
          It's just...

                    SARAH

                    Ecstasy.

                         ROBBIE
               Really? What's it like?

                         SARAH
               It's...it's like being in
               love with yourself.

                         ROBBIE
               Does it make you...

                         SARAH
               What?

                         ROBBIE

               You know?

                         SARAH

               No?

                         ROBBIE
               Uh, horny.

                         SARAH
                    (laughing)
               It depends.

          Robbie nods.

                         SARAH (CONTÍD)
          It's not as sexual as the name implies. I
          mean if you're with someone you like, it can
          be. It doesn't make you something you're
          not. It just brings out the happiness you
          have inside. You know?

           Robbie nods.

                    SARAH (CONTÍD)
          Have you ever done drugs?

                    ROBBIE
          I tried pot once. It was
          boring. But hey, aren't you
          worried? About addiction?

                    SARAH
          No, I take full
          responsibility for my
          actions. There is a
          difference between use and
          abuse. Extremes are the
          problem. And people not
          taking responsibility for
          themselves. If you want to do
          something, educate yourself
          and use common sense - don't
          drive, hang with your close
          friends, you know?

Robbie nods.

                    SARAH (CONTÍD)
          I know exactly what I'm
          doing. I'm not out of
          control. I'm not hurting
          anyone. And I feel great.

                    SARAH (CONTÍD)
          I'm really glad I met you.

                    ROBBIE
          Yeah, me, too.

                    SARAH
          Well, I think I better get
          back to my friends now.

                    ROBBIE

                    Yeah, I got get going, too.

Robbie gets up and helps Sarah up. She turns
and gives him a big hug and a kiss on the
cheek.

                         SARAH
          I'll see you around, okay?

                         ROBBIE
          Yeah, I hope so.

                         SARAH
          And good luck finding your sister.

                         ROBBIE
          Thanks.

Robbie watches as Sarah walks away.
                                        CUT TO:

EXT - PARK - NIGHT

Paz dancing in front of stage.

                         PAZ
          Isn't this great?

Alyssa looks at her, annoyed.
Andy is lying on the floor with his shirt
wrapped around his head like turban.

                         ANDY
          I can't believe this!

                         ALYSSA
          I have to go look for him.
          You guys stay here. Don't
          move! I'll be back.

Paz doesn't even hear her. Andy waves her off.

                         ANDY
               Whatever.

                                        CUT TO:

Alyssa walks away.

EXT -PARK - NIGHT

Robbie searching.

Shots of Rave as Robbie looks around.

EXT - PARK - NIGHT

Alyssa searching.

Shots of Rave as Alyssa looks.

EXT - PARK - NIGHT

Robbie sees Rolly.
                                        CUT TO:

                         ROBBIE
                         (to himself)
               Be a man.
Robbie walks over to Rolly and taps his
shoulder.

                         ROLLY
                         (drunk)
               Well, what the fuck do you
               want? Spill my beer?

                         ROBBIE
               No, you're doing just fine on
               your own.

Rolly's friends laugh.

                         ROLLY
               What did you say?

                    ROBBIE
          Look, man, I just need the
          backpack. It's not mine and I
          have to return it.

                    ROLLY
          Well, that's not my problem,
          is it?

                    ROBBIE
          Come on, help me out here.

                    ROLLY
          I ain't giving you shit so
          get the fuck out of my face.

                    ROBBIE
          Look man, I need that
          backpack.

                    ROLLY
          You need it?

Rolly grabs the backpack and holds it
up.

                    ROLLY (CONTÍD)
          Well, come and get it.

Robbie shakes his head.

                    ROLLY (CONTÍD)
          Come on...

Robbie rushes Rolly taking him down and
landing on top of him. Robbie manages to
grab the backpack.

Rolly turns him over and begins hitting him.

Robbie swings and knocks him back. He gets
up, back pack in hand.

Rolly's friends step towards him.

OFF SCREEN:

                    JUANA
          Alo, baby!

Robbie turns to see Juana.

Alex, Ivan, and Carlos step forward. Rolly's

friends step back.

Robbie walks over to Juana. Juana reaches
over and kisses Robbie.

                    JUANA (CONTÍD)
          Are you okay? Oh, my god,
          you're bleeding!

Robbie wipes blood from his nose.

                    ROBBIE
          Nah, I'm fine.

Rolly gets up, stumbling, looks at Robbie.

                    ROLLY
          I'll see you around.

                    ROBBIE
               (nodding)
          Yeah.

Robbie turns to Juana and the boys.

                    ROBBIE (CONTÍD)
          Thanks.

                    JUANA
          For what? We got here late.
          You got hurt, baby.

                    ROBBIE
          Not too bad.

                    JUANA
          You find your sister?

                    ROBBIE
          Not yet.

                    JUANA
          We're going to hear DJ Luis
          Diaz play. You want to come?

                    ROBBIE
          Thanks, but I have to go
          return this.

                    JUANA
          Okay, baby, you be careful, okay?

                    ROBBIE
          I will.

Robbie kisses Juana goodbye.

                    ROBBIE (CONTÍD)
          Bye, Juana.

                    JUANA
          Bye, mi amor.

Robbie walks away and begins searching
again.

EXT -PARK - NIGHT

Robbie stops and watches DJ Lloyd spinning.
People dancing around, having fun.
He spots Drug Dealer and walks over to him.
He taps him on the shoulder and Drug Dealer
turns around.

                    ROBBIE
               (ducking)

                    Wait, wait, here.

Drug Dealer grabs the backpack. He opens it
up and freaks out.

                    DRUG DEALER
          Where's the box?

                    ROBBIE
          What box?

                    DRUG DEALER
          The mint box.

Robbie pulls the box out of his pocket.

                    ROBBIE
             This?

Drug Dealer grabs the box. And opens it.

                    DRUG DEALER
          Did you touch them?

                    ROBBIE
               (shaking his head)
          I hate mints.

Drug Dealer grabs him, looking him straight
in the eyes. He puts him down.

                    DRUG DEALER
          Right.
               (looking at his bruises)
          What the fuck happened to
          you?

                    ROBBIE
          Life.

Drug Dealer smiles.

                    DRUG DEALER
          Rough day?

Robbie nods.

                    DRUG DEALER (CONTÍD)
          Look, I'm sorry but you stole
          my fucking bag.

                    ROBBIE
          Yeah, sorry about that.

                    DRUG DEALER
          Tell you what? We're even?

                    ROBBIE
          Alright. Even.

Drug Dealer smiles and reaches his hand out.
Robbie shakes it. Drug Dealer walks away.

Robbie looks down at his hand. He is holding
a pill. He looks back up. The Drug Dealer is
gone.

Robbie pockets the pill and begins to walk
around. Robbie walks past people dancing.

Alyssa walks into frame.

                    ALYSSA
          Robbie!

Robbie turns around and sees Alyssa.

                    ROBBIE
          Alyssa!

They run and hug each other. Then, they let
go quickly, keeping it cool.

                    ALYSSA
                  (angrily)
          Where the HELL have you been?
          We looked everywhere! I've
          been worried sick! I can't
          believe you!
Alyssa looks Robbie over. She calms down.

                 ALYSSA (CONTÍD)
          Are you okay? What happened?

                    ROBBIE
          I'm okay.

                    ALYSSA
          Let's go.

                                        CUT TO:

EXT - PARK - NIGHT

Alyssa leads Robbie over to Paz and Andy.

                    ANDY
          Finally!

                    PAZ
                  (to Alyssa)
          You totally missed DJ Lloyd.
                  (to Robbie)
          What happened to you?

Robbie goes to answer.

                    PAZ (CONTÍD)
                  (quietly)
         Oh, Alyssa, he's walking this
         way.

                    ALYSSA
         No way.
Lloyd walks over.
                    LLOYD
         Hey, Robbie.

Robbie turns to shake Lloyd's hand.

                    ROBBIE
         What's up Lloyd?

                    LLOYD
         Just finished my set. Did you
         hear me?

                    ROBBIE
         Uh, I think I just caught the
         end. Why don't you just give me
         a CD or something.

Alyssa, Paz, and Andy stare in amazement.

                    LLOYD (CONTÍD)
         You resolve that little problem?

Lloyd reaches over, looking at his bruised
face.

                    ROBBIE
         Yup, no more problem.

Lloyd looks over at Alyssa, Paz, and Andy.

                    LLOYD
         You find your sister?

                    ROBBIE
          Yeah. This is my sister,
          Alyssa. Alyssa, this is
          Lloyd.

Alyssa smiles and shakes his hand.

                    LLOYD
          Nice to meet you.

                    ALYSSA
          Yeah, nice meeting you, too.

                    ROBBIE
          This is Paz. And Andy.

Paz shakes his hand.

                    PAZ
          Your set was awesome!

                    LLOYD
          Thanks.
Andy shakes his hand.

                    ANDY
          Good to meet you.

                    LLOYD
          Likewise.
               (to Robbie)
          So, what are you gonna do
          now?

                    ROBBIE
          Ah, just hang out.

Lloyd looks over at Alyssa again.

                    LLOYD

                    Mind if I join?

                         ROBBIE
                    Nah, that's cool.

Alyssa and Paz exchange glances.

                         ANDY
                    Alright, enough! I need to
                    take my pill! NOW!

Alyssa grabs Robbie and pulls him aside.

                         ALYSSA
                    Robbie, I was wondering. If I
                    took ecstasy, would you be
                    cool with that? I mean, would
                    you tell Mom? I mean we can
                    talk about this at home. You
                    can ask me whatever you want.

Robbie smiles at Alyssa.

                         ROBBIE
                    It's cool.

                         ALYSSA
                    Really?

                         ROBBIE
                    Really.

They join the group.

                         ROBBIE (CONTÍD)
                    Actually I have one, too.
                    Long story.

Alyssa looks surprised.

They all start walking toward a stage when

Sarah comes running over to Robbie. She
throws her arms around him, hugging him.

                    SARAH
          You *are* the cutest one here.

Sarah kisses Robbie on the lips. She laughs
at his surprise.

The group watches in amazement.

                    ROBBIE
          Hey, hi, wow. I have
          something for you.

Robbie pulls out the pill and places it in
Sarah's hand.
                    SARAH
          Is this?

                    ROBBIE
          Yeah.

                    SARAH
          Oh, you don't have to. Keep
          it.

                    ROBBIE
          No, I'm not ready for that
          yet. You have it. I want you
          to.

                    SARAH
          You really don't have to.

                    ANDY
          Uh-uh, I know you're not
          fighting over who's NOT
          taking the pill.
          Party foul! One of you decide
          before I take it!

                    PAZ
          You have your own, slut!

                   ANDY
                (to Alyssa)
          Speaking of which...

                  ALYSSA
          Okay.
Alyssa and Andy, look around, toast, take
their pills, and offer water to Sarah. She
takes her pill.

                  SARAH
          Thanks, Robbie. You really
          didn't have to.

Sarah hugs Robbie.
                  ROBBIE
          I know.

OFF SCREEN:

                  JUANA

     NO!

Juana walks ON SCREEN.

                  JUANA (CONTÍD)
          I can't believe this. I leave
          you   alone   and   already   you
          cheating on me.

                  ROBBIE
          Juana!

Juana hugs Robbie.

                  Juana
          Baby, every time I see you,

                    you look worse.

Robbie laughs.

                    ROBBIE
          Juana, this is my sister,
          Alyssa. And Paz, Andy, Sarah,
          and Lloyd.

Juana kisses them all hello.

                    JUANA
               (to Lloyd)
          I recognize you, love.

                    JUANA
          This is Alex, Ivan, y Carlos.

The boys wave at everybody.

                    ANDY
               (towards the boys)
          Hello, hello.

                    JUANA
          So, you find your sister?
          Good.
               (to Alyssa)
          You have a wonderful brother,
          no?

                    ALYSSA
          Yeah, he's pretty cool.

                    JUANA
          Okay, I'm going to hear Carl
          Cox. Who's coming?

They all mumble in agreement and begin
walking towards the stage.

                    ALYSSA
                 (to Robbie)
        What did you DO today?

                    ROBBIE
        Don't ask.

Robbie puts his arm around her as they walk.

                    ALYSSA
        You know, I just want to say
        this before my pill kicks in.
        I love you.

                    ROBBIE
                  (laughing)
        Yeah, I love you, too.

SHOTS of Robbie dancing with everyone.

                  THE END

About the Movie

"A story is told three times: In the script, when you shoot it, and in the editing room."

\- Filmmaking Lore

Inception

I was in Miami when I got a call from a friend and Miami Veteran Club Promoter Bruce Braxton asking if I was available to help produce the Ultra Music Festival. It was the first year it was going to be in Downtown Miami. I said no. I was retired from that world because I became a filmmaker. He kept asking. I finally agreed on the condition that I would make a movie and shoot something during the two-day show. And so it began.

Development

I had a setting, so I just needed a story. What can happen during a music festival? So much, but getting lost sucks. (This was before everyone had a cellphone!) But, it should be someone who has no business being there. And so, Rave Alone came to life. A coming of age story about a boy who blackmails his sister into taking him to a rave. He gets lost, has an adventure, and grows up along the way.

Pre-production

The script came together quickly with my sister Paz Fernandez and soul sister Andrea Roa's instrumental help. It was magical creativity at its best. I had help—tons and tons of support. We got a crew together of friends and local professionals. We found great actors in a theater group to play the leads. Matthew Leddy played Robbie, Jennifer Lehr, his sister Alyssa, her best friends Andy and Paz were Claire Murray and Sofia Citarella.

Production

The script changed a bit, as it always does. Since we had to cut the Dad, we shot a single Mom instead. Juana, a friend of mine and a real person, couldn't do it; fortunately, the incomparable Shawn Palacious, aka Kitty Meow, played the part. The crew filled in for some of the cast that went M.I.A. with a standout performance by Assistant Director (and reluctant actor) Jamin O'Brien, who played the Drug Dealer brilliantly at the last moment going beyond the call of duty. We shot the house scenes on Friday, March 23, 2001, and all day and night on Saturday at Ultra3. The Sunday morning sun is what stopped us as we got the final moments of the fight scene.

Life-Interrupted

Life sometimes gets in the way of our passion projects. I went back to Los Angeles to work, got busy, and the movie took an extended hiatus! In one of my many cross-country moves, my production notes binder got lost.

Post Production

My dear friend and collaborator, Allen Paschel of Flinger Films, who worked one of the cameras and played the Cop, has been the Keeper of the Tapes (we shot this in Mini-DV) and the post-production one-man-show for years!

I recently found the screenplay, photos of the production, and the production folder. This is a compelling story. Hopefully, one day, this passion project will see the light of day. In the meantime, it is time to share the screenplay and our story of trying to make it come to life.

Release

Wouldn't it be great to finish it in 2021, twenty years later? All proceeds from this book will go towards completing the film. We set up a GoFundMe page to crowdsource and get help with post-production and completion of the film. All money raised will go towards finishing the film with proper sound editing and house music licensing. After that goal is met, distribution and marketing come next. If you can, please consider making a donation (no amount is too small) at gofundme.com/f/rave-alone-movie and sharing it with your friends. You can also help us by reviewing this book on Amazon. Regardless, all the best to you and yours. May stories and music inspire you, always!

Acknowledgements

This project was so much fun to work on and create. It was a glorious creative endeavor despite the time restrictions and budget constraints.

I appreciate:

- The hundreds of individuals who made this movie possible back in 2001.

- Andrea Roa and Paz Fernandez, my creative muses helping me birth this idea.

- The crew, cast, family, and friends pitched in with their talent and time.

- Allen Paschel, the co-parent of this creative baby all these years who never lost faith in this project.

- The future supporters and collaborators still to join and help finish the job.

Thank you, all!

About the Author

 Macarena Luz Bianchi wrote, produced, and directed ***Rave Alone*** in 2001. Her filmography is on IMDB. She is now a personal development coach and holistic practitioner. She's kindly known as a Fairy Godmother to her clients. Her lighthearted empowerment approach helps people tap into their glory through wonder, wellness, and wisdom. She writes fiction and non-fiction for adults and children and the occasional screenplay. www.macarenaluzb.com